My Horse Is My Guide

Written and illustrated by
Abigail Stratton

My Horse Is My Guide
Copyright © 2024 by Abigail Stratton

All rights reserved. No part of this publication may be reproduced, distributed, or transmitted in any form or by any means, including photocopying, recording, or other electronic or mechanical methods, without the prior written permission of the author, except in the case of brief quotations embodied in critical reviews and certain other non-commercial uses permitted by copyright law.

Tellwell Talent
www.tellwell.ca

ISBN
978-1-77941-779-4 (Hardcover)
978-1-77941-778-7 (Paperback)

My horse is my guide.

I see how the world looks when I sit high on my horse's back.

I can see how all the parts of the landscape fit together and I am no longer limited by what I could see on my own.

My horse helps me expand my vision.

My horse is my guide.

I know my horse will look after me, making sure I am not thrown
off by a nasty creature trying to startle my horse.

My horse stays calm and offers unconditional love to
all, no matter their previous wrongdoings.

My horse brings me safety, even when I need to face the hardest of lessons.

My horse is my guide.

I can trust my horse with all my secrets. Whether it's my deepest insecurities or my happiest moments, I know the things I share won't travel beyond my horse's ears.

My horse allows me to express all of who I am without fear of being rejected.

My horse is my guide.

When all my human friends stop speaking to me, I know
I will always have a friend in my horse.

My horse understands how I feel and never expects me to explain myself when I
have no words—instead, my heart races when my horse takes me somewhere new.

My horse is my guide.

Even when I am tired, my horse takes me anywhere.

When my eyes close for the night, we escape to the most beautiful places.

My horse is my guide.

My horse always comes when I call, ready to listen, ready to answer all my burning questions, and ready to help me see what I couldn't see before.

Even if we are physically apart, we are still together in spirit.

About the Author

Abigail is fascinated by the relationship between art and spiritual healing. She uses art to intuitively process life experiences and gain deeper insight into the spiritual reality we all share.

As well as being a writer and artist, Abigail is a certified master energy healer and reader. She loves facilitating an environment where clients can receive the insights they need to unlock their full potential. Helping others brings her great joy.

My Horse Is My Guide is Abigail's first book. She hopes to empower readers in the knowledge that the spiritual world is here to support and uplift us all.

www.ingramcontent.com/pod-product-compliance
Lightning Source LLC
LaVergne TN
LVHW071733060526
838200LV00031B/489